Victoria 1000 X 5
Children's Book Recycling Project

Did you know? Creating the habit of nightly bedtime reading "adds up" to this: By the time your child enters school, they will hear stories from 1000 books or more! Read to your child each day and begin literacy development, a stronger connection to you, and a lifetime love of books.

Please accept this gift of a book as a reminder of the importance of reading to young children and help support our goal—that all children in Victoria will have at least a thousand books read to them before they enter Kindergarten.

www.1000X5.ca

The *Victoria "1000 X 5" Children's Book Recycling Project* is a partnership with Greater Victoria School District #61.

Thanks: Raise-a-Reader, Rotary, ORCA Books, Santas Anonymous, Victoria Foundation

MEDIA

The Two Trees

Written by Qi Zhi

Illustrated by Cong Wei

CARDINAL MEDIA

There once was a big, big tree
with branches that were home
to a bird family.

Sometimes its fruit fell to the ground, where ants and worms would eat it.

The fruit's seeds would be planted
and sprout into new trees.

"Hello!" said one new little tree to another.

But his voice was too
soft to be heard.

The second young tree tried to wave her hands, but they were too small to be seen.

The two young trees
hoped they would
grow up quickly.

They stretched out
their hands,

but they could not
reach one another.

"We'll grow up soon,"
they thought.

Day by day, the two young trees grew taller and taller.

As they grew, she
hoped to touch
his face,

but he was still out of reach.

They tried again to hold hands,

but it seemed impossible.

"We'll have to wait until we grow taller," they said.

Finally their hands met!
They were so happy!

They waited
through winter.

By spring they
could whisper
to each other.

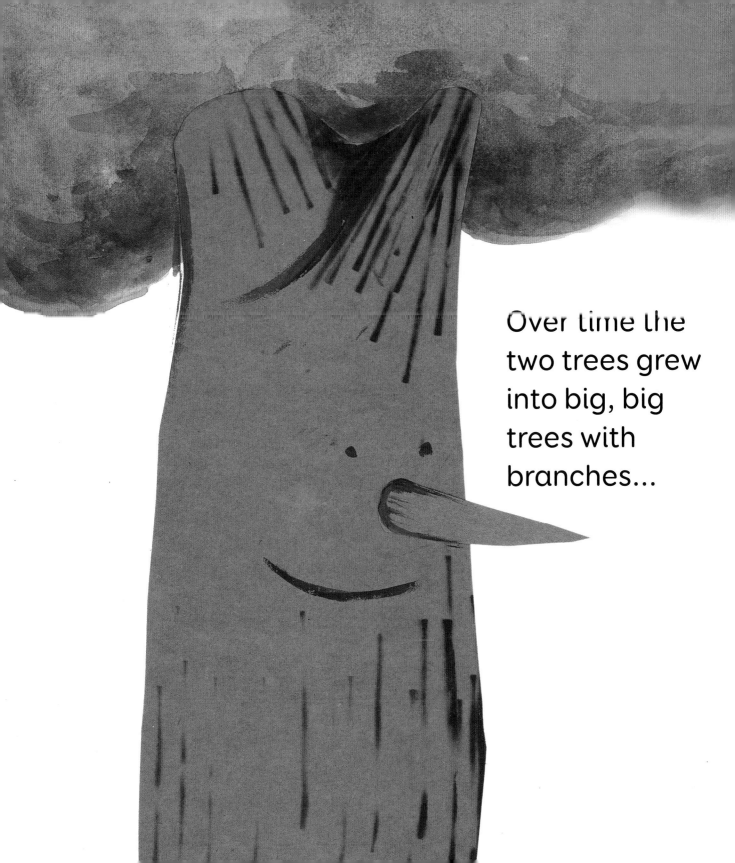

Over time the
two trees grew
into big, big
trees with
branches...

...that became home to a bird family.